Monty – up to his neck in trouble

Colin West

Collins

This edition produced for The Book People Ltd
Hall Wood Avenue, Haydock
St Helens WA11 9UL

First published in by A & C Black Ltd in 1991
Published by Young Lions in 1992
and reprinted in Collins in 1995
15 14 13 12 11 10 9 8
Collins an imprint of HarperCollins*Publishers* Ltd,
77-85 Fulham Palace Road, London W6 8JB.

The HarperCollins website address is
www.fireandwater.com

ISBN 0-00-763093-X

Monty's Toothache

One morning Monty, the dog who
wears glasses, had a bad dream.
He dreamt that all his teeth fell out
just as he was about to bite into
a juicy steak.

It was terrible!
Monty didn't have a tooth left in
his head.

Then, in his dream, a mad professor
(who looked a bit like his owner,
Mr Sprod) fitted him with a set of
false teeth.

The story even made the evening
paper, the *Nightmare News*.

MONTY–
THE DOG WHO
WEARS DENTURES

Local dog Monty has been
fitted with a revolutionary
device – a set of false teeth.
The new gnashers are the
brainchild of Prof. Sprodski,
who replaced Monty's original
when they fell out.

Monty shows off his n...

Monty woke up in a cold sweat.
He was relieved to find it was all a
dream, but he had the most
dreadful toothache
all the same.

Maybe my
teeth really
are about to
fall out!

'How awful!' thought Monty.
'Maybe I'll have to wear false teeth
in real life.'
There would be no more steaks
or toffees or bones or biscuits.

Monty was so worried he couldn't
touch his breakfast.

He couldn't even be tempted by his favourite chocolate biscuits.

The pain went on all day and just wouldn't go away.

We're worried about Monty, Dad.

In the end, Mr Sprod decided Monty
would have to visit the vet.

The waiting room made Monty feel
even worse.

He sat between a sick parrot and
a lizard covered in spots.

At last it was Monty's turn.
Mr Sprod explained what was wrong.

The vet prodded and probed Monty
for a full five minutes.
Monty didn't enjoy it.

Then the vet decided to take a look inside Monty's mouth.

Accidentally Monty nipped her fingers.

Monty's ears pricked up.

Suddenly Monty was full of beans.
He started wagging his tail and
licked the vet's hand to show that
he was sorry.

As they said goodbye, Monty forgot
about his toothache.
'I wonder what's for dinner?' he
thought. 'I haven't had a bite all day.'

Monty at the Movies

It was a wet afternoon and Mrs Sprod and the children were out shopping with Monty.

'Look!' cried Simon, 'The cinema is showing *The Four-Eyed Monster From Mars!*'

'Hey, Mum, it's about to begin – can we go in?' pleaded Josie.

'Oh, all right,' said Mrs Sprod.

I suppose it will get us out of the rain. But keep quiet about Monty – I don't think they like dogs!

Mrs Sprod bought the tickets.
Luckily the cashier didn't notice
Monty . . .

Neither did the usherette . . .

They settled in the front row.
Monty snuggled down under a seat.
Before long the lights dimmed and
everyone held their breath, waiting
for the film.

First of all there were a few adverts.
One went like this:

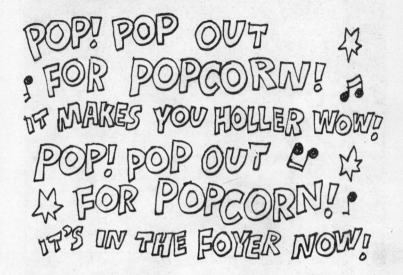

The words really got into Monty's
brain.

Soon he was in a trance.

Dreamily Monty wandered off into the darkness.

He headed up the aisle. Monty could still hear those words in his head . . .

No one noticed Monty, as by now the film had begun.

THE FOUR-EYED MONSTER FROM MARS

But Monty was hypnotised.

He could see a
bright light in the
distance, and was
drawn towards it.

When Monty
reached the
back row,
he leapt up
on an empty
seat, and
then onto
the wall
behind it.

He walked along, getting closer
and closer to the light.
Suddenly Monty was dazzled.
At the same moment, the whole
audience gasped.
Silhouetted on the huge screen
were Monty's monstrous features.

Monty came out of his trance.
He blinked a lot, toppled from his
perch, and landed on someone's lap.

'It's the Four-Eyed Monster from
Mars!' cried her boyfriend, running
away.

Everyone turned round.
Monty hardly knew where he was.
He jumped from one seat to another,
scattering people as he went.

When Monty reached the front row,
Simon and Josie caught hold of him.

'Quick, we'd better leave before we get thrown out,' whispered Mrs Sprod.

In the daylight Josie sighed: 'Huh, Monty really spoiled the film.'

'Oh well,' said Mrs Sprod, 'at least it's stopped raining now. Let's head for home.'

As they passed a sweet shop, Simon suggested: 'Can we pop in for something, Mum?'

'Pop!' thought Monty . . .

Monty's Party Adventure

Simon and Josie were off to their
friend Fiona's birthday party.

Monty knew all about parties.
He knew there was always lots of
food — sausage rolls, crisps,
sandwiches, and best of all,
chocolate cake covered in icing.

When Josie and Simon had left, Monty tried to settle down, but he couldn't help thinking of all that delicious party food.

Fiona lives just round the corner.

I'm sure she wouldn't mind me paying a surprise visit.

If I put on my 'sorrowful look,' she's bound to give me some birthday cake!

Monty's mouth was watering.
He sneaked out the back door.

He climbed on to the dustbin and
clambered over the fence.

Then he crossed next-door's garden,
and burrowed under a hedge,

and then went past a funny statue,

and then hopped on to a wheelbarrow
and leapt over a wall.

Then Monty went across the next garden, and squeezed through a gap.

Monty got a bit entangled in a washing line in the next garden.
He had to shake off a tea towel which fell on his head.

But soon he was off again, heading for a hole in the hedge.

Monty squeezed through and
wandered on to a neatly cut lawn.

He trampled over a flower bed and
made his way to the big house
at the top of the garden.

Monty guessed where Fiona and her guests would be and went up to a window. He could just make out some figures sitting at a table.

Monty tried to get a better view.

But what Monty didn't know was
that he was at the wrong house.

He'd gone wrong when the tea towel
fell on him. He was now at
Mrs Perkins-Smythe's house, where
she was giving a tea party.

Just then, Mrs Perkins-Smythe caught sight of Monty's nose pressed against the window pane.

Before Monty could run off, the vicar
ran outside and caught hold of his
collar.

'Look who I've caught!' the vicar
said triumphantly on his return.

At last Monty realised he was at the wrong house.

But soon everyone was crowding round him and feeding him cakes.

Monty had a nice snooze until
finally the guests thought it was
time to leave.

It's been lovely!

'Please allow me to return Monty,'
volunteered the vicar.
'Yes, by all means,' replied
Mrs Perkins-Smythe.

The vicar left with Monty under his
arm. As he was at the front gate,
he bumped into Josie and Simon.

They had just come from Fiona's
house nearby, and were on their
way home.

The vicar explained how Monty had brightened up the tea party.

'Thanks for looking after him,' said Josie.

'You're most welcome,' replied the vicar. 'Now goodbye, children, and goodbye to you too, Monty.'

What a kind man – it must be the 'dog collar'!

Monty at the Park

One hot summer's day, Simon, Josie and Monty went to the park to feed the ducks.

When they reached the lake, Simon
tied the end of Monty's lead to a tree.

Simon and Josie went to the water's edge and started throwing crusts. Soon they were surrounded by lots of ducks.

Meanwhile Monty was getting bored. He'd sniffed the tree, and walked round it four times. Now there didn't seem much else to do.

Monty sat in the shade and looked
longingly at the ice cream stand in
the distance.
He started licking his lips at the
thought of an ice cream.
But how could he get one?

People kept passing by, licking ices.
Monty was getting more and more
thirsty . . .

On the horizon he saw a man carrying
a soft ice cream that looked as if it
might melt at any moment.

Monty began to drool.

The ice cream grew bigger . . .

. . . and bigger . . . .

. . . AND BIGGER!

Monty jumped up to snatch a lick.

Just at that moment Monty's lead jerked up and the man tripped head over heels.

The ice cream flew out of its cone . . .

. . . and straight down Monty's throat.

Mmmm . . . it was strawberry –
Monty's favourite!

As the man brushed himself down,
Monty noticed he looked rather angry.

Just then, Josie and Simon came back from feeding the ducks. 'You should keep that dog under control!' the man shouted, before storming off.

Monty in Trouble

One Monday morning after Simon
and Josie had gone to school,
Mrs Sprod noticed Josie had left her
recorder behind.

Oh dear, that means Josie won't be able to join in Music Practice.

Monty looked sadly at the recorder
and started thinking . . .

When Mrs Sprod wasn't looking,
Monty took Josie's recorder in his
mouth and crept out of the house.

Monty had visited School before, so
he knew the way, and he raced
along the streets.

As Monty reached School, he saw the
Headmistress, Mrs Prendlethorpe,
at the entrance. She was looking out
for latecomers.

Monty found an open door, but as soon as he entered, he heard someone shout:

A woman waving a ladle started chasing Monty.

Monty jumped up on a table, and dashed along a work top, then tried to leap over a big pot.

But he didn't make it.

He fell in up to his neck.

Josie's recorder sank to the bottom,
as Monty splashed about frantically.

At last Monty scrambled out and
darted through the nearest door.

Just then the Headmistress came to see what the commotion was about. 'A funny dog got into the custard,' explained a dinner lady.

Mrs Prendlethorpe's face dropped.

Mrs Prendlethorpe realised it could only be Monty.

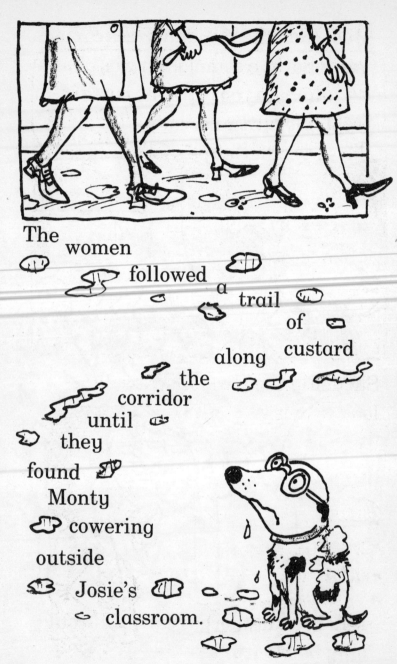

The women followed a trail of custard along the corridor until they found Monty cowering outside Josie's classroom.

Mrs P. asked Josie to explain things.

I'm sorry, Miss, but Monty has a knack of putting his foot in it.

He put more than just his foot in today's custard!

Suddenly the Headmistress didn't look so cross.

Hmm... that means we won't be able to have pudding at dinner-time.

HEALTHY EATING FOR KIDS by Vita Mins

Mrs Prendlethorpe went away looking much happier.

A little later, at dinner-time, she announced that everyone would have fresh fruit today instead of pudding.

A lot of children found they preferred
fruit . . .

Mrs Prendlethorpe was so pleased,
she even fished out Josie's recorder
and cleaned it up so Josie could join
in with Music Practice after all.

Then Mrs Prendlethorpe phoned
Mrs Sprod to tell her that Monty was
safe and sound, and gave him his very
own lunch – a nice healthy apple.

64